Leaving the Nest

Mordicai Gerstein

FRANCES FOSTER BOOKS
FARRAR, STRAUS AND GIROUX
NEW YORK

"The world is big and scary,"
says Baby Jay. "There are cats and giants.
I will never leave this cozy nest!"

"Tomorrow I'm leaving this nest!" says Baby Squirrel.

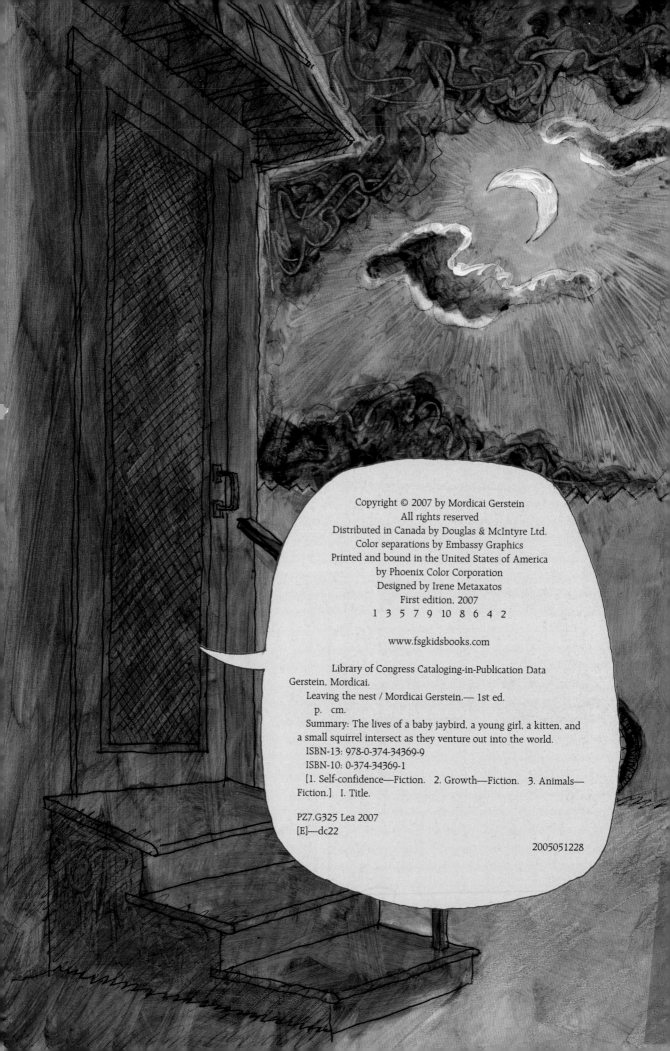

Distributed in Canada by Douglas & McIntyre Ltd.
Color separations by Embassy Graphics
Printed and bound in the United States of America
by Phoenix Color Corporation
Designed by Irene Metaxatos
First edition, 2007
1 3 5 7 9 10 8 6 4 2

www.fsgkidsbooks.com

Library of Congress Cataloging-in-Publication Data
Gerstein, Mordicai.
    Leaving the nest / Mordicai Gerstein.— 1st ed.
        p.   cm.
    Summary: The lives of a baby jaybird, a young girl, a kitten, and
a small squirrel intersect as they venture out into the world.
    ISBN-13: 978-0-374-34369-9
    ISBN-10: 0-374-34369-1
    [1. Self-confidence—Fiction.   2. Growth—Fiction.   3. Animals—
Fiction.]   I. Title.

PZ7.G325 Lea 2007
[E]—dc22
                                                                    2005051228